Other Books by
R.L. STINE

SERIES:

- Goosebumps
- Fear Street
- Rotten School
- Mostly Ghostly

INDIVIDUAL TITLES:

- *It's the First Day of School…Forever!*
- *The Haunting Hour*
- *The Nightmare Hour*
- *Zombie Town*
- *The Adventures of Shrinkman*
- *The 13th Warning*
- *Three Faces of Me*
- *My Alien Parents*

THE CREATURES FROM BEYOND BEYOND

Text copyright © 2000 Parachute Press
Cover illustration by Tim Jacobus

A Parachute Press Book

Published by Amazon Publishing
P.O. Box 400818
Las Vegas, NV 89140

ISBN-13: 9781612183275
ISBN-10: 1612183271

R.L. STINE

THE CREATURES FROM BEYOND BEYOND

amazonpublishing

INTRODUCTION

· R.L. STINE ·

I admit it. This is a strange book.

It starts out with something I love to write about—an evil doll that comes to life. Then it moves on to giant, ferocious space lizards that invade Earth. And then the story is about battling someone controlling your mind. Poor Randi, our narrator, is being controlled by an alien from outer space.

You get a little bit of everything in this book—and it's ALL scary!

Let's start with the evil doll. I've written so many books and stories about dolls and puppets and dummies that come to life. It's something I found frightening even as a kid. Even as a *very young* kid.

When I was three, I had to take a nap in the afternoon. And before each nap, my mother would read a chapter of a book to me. One of the books she read was the original *Pinocchio*.

I'm not sure why she picked this book—because it scared me to death!

The original *Pinocchio* book is very violent. Pinocchio takes a big wooden mallet and *smashes* the cricket flat against the wall. Then poor Pinocchio falls asleep with his feet on the stove. Remember? He's a wooden puppet? Well, he *burns his feet off*!

I was only three, but I never forgot that scene. I think that's why I've found puppets and dummies and dolls scary ever since. And I think a lot of other people find them scary too.

My most popular Goosebumps villain is definitely Slappy, the evil dummy. When someone says the mysterious words KARRU MARRI ODONNA LOMA MOLONU KARRANO, Slappy opens his painted eyes and comes to life.

Slappy is so popular that I've written seven books about him, starting with *Night of the Living Dummy*. Right now I'm working on a new book called *Son of Slappy*, and I'm sure the son will be just as terrifying as his dad.

When Randi and Tyler, the twins in *The Creatures from Beyond Beyond*, move into their summer house, they find a pile of old dolls in a bedroom. Will one of the dolls come to life? You can bet on it. And as in all these stories, it will *not* be nice!

Where did I get the idea for this book? I have an office in my apartment in New York City where I write my books. One day I was sitting at my desk staring at the movie posters on my wall. I have several posters of old horror movies that inspire me.

Some of the posters on my wall are:

- ATTACK OF THE CRAB MONSTERS
- THE CREATURE WALKS AMONG US
- THE DEADLY MANTIS
- TARANTULA!
- ATTACK OF THE GIANT LEECHES
- THE CREATURE FROM THE BLACK LAGOON

Everyone loved monster movies when I was a kid. Monster insects were most popular. But movie audiences also loved monster birds, monster lizards, monster gorillas, monster sea creatures. And just plain ugly *monsters* who didn't look like any Earth creature at all!

Everyone likes a good scare. The first—and maybe most popular—movie monster was King Kong. *King Kong* was made in 1933 and started the mania for big, *biiiig* monsters.

Audiences had never seen anything like King Kong. The audience tingled with fear when the explorers on an unknown jungle island saw King Kong, the gigantic gorilla, for the first time. And when the mile-high gorilla reached down and picked up the woman in the group and kidnapped her, audiences screamed.

The film was so popular that it led to *Son of Kong* later in 1933 and *Mighty Joe Young* in 1947, a film about another gigantic gorilla. Since then there have been many *King Kong* remakes and sequels.

Why? Because who doesn't like to see an enormous imaginary creature destroy everything in its path?

Audiences loved watching King Kong loose in New York City, stomping on cars and buildings and grabbing trains off their tracks. In the 1950s, Japanese moviemakers got into the destruction act with their own huge monsters. *Godzilla* and *Rodan* stomped all over Tokyo. And movie fans all over the world went wild for them.

When my brother Bill and I were kids, we went to see a horror movie nearly every Sunday afternoon. The movies were slower in those days. You had to wait a *long* time before the monster appeared on the screen. But when it finally stomped or flew or swam onto the screen, we all went nuts, screaming and jumping up and down and cheering the monster on.

Those are great memories for me. And as I sat in my office staring at my movie posters, a title popped into my head: THE CREATURES FROM BEYOND BEYOND.

I loved the title. It sounded just like all the movies I loved as a kid—with a little bit of a funny twist.

I wrote the title down. And then I started to think up the story. Dolls coming to life…ugly monsters from outer space…weird mind control. It's all here. Hope it scares you!

RL Stine

CHAPTER 1

I walked up the front stairs of our latest "summer place." Every year for summer vacation, my family goes someplace *new*. Which doesn't necessarily mean someplace *good*.

"I have first dibs on a room!" Tyler yelled, knocking me over as he raced up the front steps.

"No fair!" I shouted, chasing him into the house.

Tyler and I are twins. We both have curly brown hair and gray-blue eyes. It's easy to tell us apart, though. That's because Tyler is a boy and I'm a girl.

I reached the top of the stairs.

Tyler had already thrown open all the doors. As he looked into the last room at the end of the hall, he let out an ear-shattering shriek.

I rushed up next to him. "What's wrong?"

"Nothing! This one's awesome. And it's mi-ine!" he chanted. I peered into the room. Monster masks on the wall, cartoon characters on the bedspread, and sketches of comic-book heroes tacked up on the corkboard over the desk. A totally cool room!

"That one can be yours, Randi!" He waved his hand at the other room.

I looked inside it.

Ugh. Dolls. A whole wall of them! Old-fashioned dolls, tickle-me dolls, staring dolls with gleaming glass eyes, baby dolls, troll dolls, even a couple of turtles in karate gear.

I hate dolls. They creep me out. Tyler knows it.

He is *such* a jerk sometimes.

He knew I would never be able to talk Mom and Dad into making Tyler live in a room full of dolls so I could have the cool room. Our parents try to be fair, but even they have their limits.

"You are so totally taking advantage of me being a girl," I muttered.

Tyler shrugged and tried not to smirk.

I checked out the other open doors on the upstairs landing.

Master bedroom. Mom and Dad would sleep there. It had a big closet with a window. They could put my little brother Alex's bed in there. He was four and didn't need a big room to himself.

Next was a bathroom with a shower-tub combo. I glanced through the bathroom window. A big house stood next door—no curtains on the windows, no furniture in the rooms. Vacant, I guessed.

There were two closed doors in the upstairs hallway. One had a sign taped to it that said OFF LIMITS in dripping Halloween letters, and the other opened to reveal a linen closet.

No other bedrooms. I was definitely stuck in Doll-land.

Every summer my family switches houses with some other family in another town. I wouldn't mind spending the summer in L.A. with my friends, but when I ask, Mom and Dad always say no.

Other families totally want to switch houses with *us* so they can go to Disneyland and Universal Studios and the La Brea Tar Pits and other stuff I've seen a hundred times.

And I have to admit, we've seen some terrific things living in different places. Like the year we stayed in New Mexico and went to Carlsbad Caverns. Coolest caves I've ever seen.

Tyler and I took turns videotaping Carlsbad. We're working on a horror movie together. At twilight, tons of bats come whooshing out of the caves. It's totally scary!

My other favorite was the summer in New Orleans. *Everything* in New Orleans is weird. Tyler and I got some terrific cemetery footage. So why were we in Blairingville this summer?

Blairingville. It should be called Boringville!

Dad said it would give us a feel for small-town living. Too bad I had zero interest in small-town living.

So far I hadn't seen a single thing that excited me. Just a bunch of identical houses, streets, trees, and summerbrown lawns. Oh, and a totally dinky mall. Nothing like the Galleria at home.

I dropped my duffel bag on the doll-room floor and sighed.

I wanted to throw a sheet over those dolls so I wouldn't have to see them every minute of the day and night.

"Wow!" A voice came from the doorway.

I turned and saw Mom standing there. "Oh, wow!" she said again.

"Museum," piped my little brother Alex from beside her. He stared wide-eyed at the dolls.

"It's not a museum, it's a *nightmare*—" I began. Then I glanced at Mom.

Her eyes went soft as she stared at all those plastic people on the shelf. "So beautiful," she whispered, coming into the room and picking up a doll dressed in velvet and lace. She touched its cheek, then its tumble of brown curls.

"You and Dad can have this room," I offered. "I'll take care of Alex!"

Mom glared at me, her eyebrows lowered.

"It was just a suggestion," I grumbled.

She put the doll back. "Be sure you don't play

with these, Randi," she said. "They belong to someone else."

I stuck my index finger in my open mouth and made a gagging noise. Playing with dolls? No chance.

Mom patted me on the head and left the room. Alex followed, clinging to her pant leg.

We unpacked and went out for pizza. Later, we all settled in for our first night in Blairingville.

Going to bed in a strange place is always a little uncomfortable. But this place was weirder than I expected. As I took my nightgown from the drawer, I felt someone staring at me.

I whirled around. The dolls! Everywhere I went in the room the dolls seemed to stare right at me. My imagination was totally getting away with me. I jumped under the sheet and clicked off the lamp as quickly as I could.

Lying in the darkness, I could feel those creepy doll eyes on me. I pulled the sheet up over my head and tried to fall asleep.

No use. I lay awake tossing and turning for hours. *That's it*, I thought. I've had enough. I clicked on the light and glared at the dolls from my bed.

When I really focused I could tell that most of them just had dull dusty eyes that didn't see anything. Then I noticed something—a doll on the top shelf that bugged me.

It was a boy doll that looked like it was supposed to be about twelve years old, which was totally weird. I mean, who ever heard of a twelve-year-old boy doll?

I glanced over at the dolls next to him and—hey, wait a minute! Had the boy doll's eyes just shifted?

It couldn't be—but I decided that he would be better off in the closet for the night, anyway. I got the desk chair and dragged it over to the shelves. I climbed up onto it and stood face-to-face with the boy doll.

Whoa. This doll looked totally real. It was only eight inches tall, but he had real blond hair, gleaming blue eyes, a lopsided smile. He even had actual eyebrows instead of painted-on ones.

His clothes had great details, too. He wore a green-and-white striped shirt and blue jeans, and his jeans had tiny rivets on the pockets. His black-and-white sneakers had real laces. Creepy! But also, kind of…neat.

Whatever. I didn't want that thing watching me while I slept. I hesitated, then grabbed it. It felt so... warm!

My finger touched the back of the doll's neck. I felt something weird—a little sticky patch. Yuck! Was it chewing gum?

I touched it again—

And the doll moved in my hand.

CHAPTER 2

It moved!

I gave a little scream. My first impulse was to throw the doll across the room. But I went with my second impulse and just held on tight. If I broke something in someone else's house, Dad would never let me hear the end of it.

The doll had moved! I stared at him.

No, wait. He hadn't moved. He had *grown*. He was twice as big as he had been just a second before. I was sure of it.

"Hey!" someone yelled in my ear.

I spun around in shock. Tyler.

"Cut it out," I growled. I gave his shoulder a shove.

"I heard you moving around in here," he said. "What's going on?"

I took a deep breath, then got down off the chair, still holding the doll.

"You have to see this," I said, my voice coming out all shaky. "It's really weird."

Tyler glanced toward the door of our parents' room. All clear. He closed the door behind him.

"What is it?" he asked.

I set the doll carefully on the quilt on the bed. "Look."

"What? It's just a dumb doll."

I turned the doll facedown and brushed the silky hair away from the back of his neck. Where was that sticky spot?

Right there. A square black patch on the neck.

"Watch this," I said. I touched the black spot.

The doll's size doubled again!

"Whoa!" Tyler yelped. "Too cool!"

My brother and I spend a lot of time prowling

the Toys "R" Us aisles and we'd never seen any-thing as awesome as this!

We both pressed the black spot on the doll. It grew again.

Tyler and I glanced at each other. Then we pounced on the doll, tapping the black patch as fast as we could.

With each growth spurt my doll looked more real. Soon it was almost my size!

I tapped once more, and the doll grew bigger than I was. I stretched myself to tap his neck one more time.

I reached for the black patch...and the doll turned over—by itself! He stared up at me with his blue eyes—and grabbed my wrist.

I gasped. My eyes widened with surprise.

The doll-boy tightened its grip. "What are you doing?" he asked.

CHAPTER 3

Ow! His grip on my wrist hurt.

I couldn't believe it. This *was* happening! That doll turned into an actual kid!

I stared at him in shock. He had blond hair, blue eyes, a California tan, and zero zits. He was just like somebody on the cover of one of those teen magazines my friend Roxanne started bringing to school, I realized.

And he was breathing!

I glanced at my brother. Tyler had a look of total shock on his face.

The doll-boy dropped my wrist. "Who are you?" he asked me.

I slid off the bed and stepped away from him toward my brother.

Whoa! What *was* this doll? I wondered. A person? A robot? And where could it have come from?

Tyler stood watching, his mouth still half open.

The boy glared at us. His eyes looked totally cold.

I thought for a second about that horror movie where a doll comes to life and goes around slicing up everybody.

Was this *that* kind of doll?

I flexed my wrist. It still hurt from the doll's grip.

"Or, I guess the real question is, what am I going to do with you?" the doll-boy muttered.

CHAPTER 4

My heart pounded. What did he mean? What *was* he going to do with us? A knock sounded on the door.

"Randi! It's the middle of the night. Why are you up?" Mom muttered through the door. "And don't pretend you're asleep! I can see the light under your door."

"Mom!" I yelled.

"Shh," Mom hissed through the door. "Not so loud! Don't wake Alex. It took him hours to get to sleep!"

The boy stared at me and Tyler again. He slid off the bed and dropped on his belly to the floor.

What was he doing?

The boy reached under the bed. I heard a weird, faint, high noise. It sounded kind of like a dentist's drill, but muffled.

What was that?

"Randi?" Mom muttered.

Should I answer her? I wondered. Should I not?

Tyler bit his lower lip. Slowly, softly, he knelt beside the boy and jabbed two fingers at the sticky patch on the boy's neck!

The boy froze in position and *shrank!* I wiped my forehead with my arm. I hadn't even realized I was sweating.

"How did you know you could do that?" I asked.

"I didn't," Tyler admitted. "Just luck." Tyler tapped the boy's neck like a madman, and then...

There was nothing but a doll lying on the floor.

"RANDI!" Mom could sure sound loud when she was talking softly!

"Mom?" Still shaky, I wobbled over and opened the door.

"What are you two doing?" she demanded. She walked into the room.

"Heh-heh." Tyler gave a half-hearted laugh. He held up the shrunken boy. "Just playing with dolls."

Mom looked like steam was going to shoot out of her ears. "How many rules can you break at one time?" she snapped.

Dad, shaggy and rumpled in his striped pajamas, ambled to the doorway and glanced in. He yawned behind his hand.

"First, lights out means lights out," Mom recited. "Second, there's no playing with other people's things unless you get permission. And Tyler, you should be in your own room and in bed."

"Helen," Dad said, yawning again. "It's their first night in a new place. It's summer. They're almost twelve. Don't you think we should relax a little?"

Mom's shoulders sagged. "Well…maybe," she muttered. "Okay. Kids, it's lights out for real now. You can explore tomorrow. But leave those dolls alone!"

She grabbed the boy doll and put him back on the shelf. Fortunately, she faced him toward the wall. "C'mon, Tyler, clear out of here." Mom made shooing motions at him with her hands.

"But—" Tyler and I said at the same time. His gaze met mine. I knew what he was thinking. We had to talk about what just happened. We had to figure out what went on here!

"Kids," Dad said in the voice that meant he was about to get serious. "Save it."

I sketched a *T* in the air with my index finger, and Tyler nodded. It's one of our things. *T* means "tomorrow." We'd talk about it then.

I still had trouble falling asleep after everyone left.

Questions kept running through my brain— what just happened? Who *was* that guy? *What* was that guy? A robot? A doll? What did he want?

And the most important question of all—What if he could grow while I was asleep?

I realized I was wrong about Blairingville. This place was a *total* horror show. And my first day here was going to keep me awake all night.

I must have slept, because the next thing I knew, it was morning.

What a weird dream, I thought, stretching my body out to its full length. I lifted my hands in front of me. A shadowy bruise bracelet circled my right wrist.

I closed my eyes for a minute and remembered the doll-boy—the way he had grabbed my wrist.

There was no denying it. What happened last night was real.

I checked the dolls. The grow-boy was still where Mom had left him, facing the wall among the antique-looking dolls. I could see the black patch on the back of his neck.

I peered at the backs of the necks of some of the other dolls. I didn't discover any more of the black patches.

I wanted to check out the growing doll again, but no way was I going to do it alone. I needed Tyler.

I got dressed and headed downstairs. The smell of Dad's special pancakes frying drifted in from the kitchen. Yum!

When I got to the table everybody else was already there and eating. Mom and Dad were dressed in their jogging outfits.

Yeow! Every time they wore those things, I felt like I needed sunglasses just to look at them. Pink. Purple. Lime green. Banana yellow. Total death by embarrassment.

Alex sat in his high chair, talking to himself and smooshing syrupy pancake pieces with his fork.

I stared at Tyler until he looked back at me. This never takes long. We can usually feel it when one of us is looking at the other, even when we're facing in totally opposite directions.

"Did that?" he said. Meaning: *Did what I remember really happen last night?*

"It did," I said.

"I don't—" he answered. Meaning: *I don't believe it.*

"Well, do," I said. I reached for my knife and fork, flashing Tyler my bruised wrist. His eyes widened.

Dad smirked at us. "Will you two stop with the secret twin language!"

"Later," Tyler and I muttered at the same time.

The two of us cleared the table after breakfast and washed the dishes. Then Mom and Dad left for their morning jog-around-and-let-the-neighbors-make-fun-of-us-in-these-crazy-outfits expedition.

As soon as the coast was clear, I settled Alex in the living room with a bunch of blocks and Tyler and I went to find out more about the dolls.

We reached the upstairs hall and were about to go into my room when I heard something.

Skritch scratch skritch.

I grabbed Tyler's arm.

Skritch.

Where was that coming from?

We both peered all around.

Scratch scratch…

There! It was coming from the closet. The one with the big OFF LIMITS sign on the door.

This was a house where totally sick and possibly dangerous dolls were sitting right out in the open! I thought. What horrible thing could possibly be in a closet that said "off limits"? I wasn't sure I wanted to find out.

Yooowww!

Another noise sounded from behind the door.

The hair on the back of my neck prickled. My heart speeded.

ROOOOOOWWWWL!

I'd never heard a sound so scary in my life!

No doubt about it. Something terrible—something horrible—something *alive* was sitting on the other side of that door!

CHAPTER 5

YaaarrrrOOWWWL!

"Let's get out of here!" I told Tyler. I raced down the stairs and into the living room.

"Grab Alex," Tyler commanded. I lifted up my little brother and lugged him out the front door.

Tyler raced right behind me. "Move! Move!" he shouted.

We ran halfway down the block before we glanced around.

Not a cloud in the bright blue sky. A sprinkler chattered out streams of water, wetting a lawn. A lawn mower mowed somewhere out of sight, and birds chirped in a big tree. Some kid came whizzing by on a bike.

Normal life. All around. Nothing scary in sight.

I glanced back at "our" house. From this distance it looked a lot like all the other houses on the street. Totally normal.

"What?" Alex tapped my face. "What? What? What?"

I set my little brother on the ground.

"Why'd you grab me?" he asked. "Huh, huh, huh?"

"There's—" I turned to Tyler for help. "There's something in the upstairs closet."

"Something making horrible noises," Tyler added.

"A monster?" Alex's eyes widened. "A monster?"

Tyler and I stared at each other. What should we say?

"I want a monster!" Alex shouted. "I want a monster! I WANT A MONSTER!"

Alex gave his most ferocious frown. Then he let out a big growl. Cute.

"Maybe we better go back," Tyler said after a little while. "Standing around like this is dumb."

"Yeah. It's daylight," I pointed out. "In horror movies most of the really scary stuff happens at night. After a power outage."

We walked back. "Mon-ster, mon-ster, mon-ster," Alex chanted with every step. I don't know about Tyler, but I felt embarrassed. Spooked by some dumb noise in a closet. Sheesh.

We went inside and stood quietly in the front hall, listening.

Skritch. Scratch. The sound again! Then—*Muurrrrow!*

Muurrrow? I thought, what kind of scary noise was *that?*

We climbed the stairs a step at a time, then stood in front of the closet door.

"Stand back here," I told Alex, setting him by the doorway into my room. "If something scary comes out, rush into my room and slam the door."

Alex frowned, sticking out his lower lip.

"Just do it!" I used my best big sister voice.

Tyler went to his room and came back with a baseball bat. He stood with the bat on his shoulder, ready to swing.

We nodded at each other, and I grabbed the door handle. I turned it and pulled, ready to jump back.

But the door was locked.

Duh, I thought. Of course a door marked OFF LIMITS would be locked.

Then again, there was probably a key somewhere around here, unless the family that lived here took it with them.

I grabbed Alex's hand, and we headed for the kitchen.

In most of the summer houses we visited, people kept spare keys in the kitchen. In one house there was even a little cupboard for them, with hooks that had labels below them telling what the keys unlocked.

In this kitchen Tyler found a drawer full of assorted junk.

In it was a key ring loaded with keys of different shapes and sizes.

We climbed the stairs again and headed for the closet door. Tyler found the right key after five tries.

We unlocked the door, then stepped back. I flung the door open. Tyler stood poised to bonk whatever came out.

Something small and gray shot out of the closet and streaked down the stairs. It went so fast I could not see what it was.

At the closed front door, though, it stopped.

It's just a cat! I thought. A skinny gray cat!

It mewed and scratched at the front door.

I ran downstairs and opened the door. The cat disappeared into the bushes.

"Did they leave the cat locked in the closet?" Tyler asked. "How *could* they?"

"And how come it didn't start making noise until this morning?" I wondered.

We peeked into the closet. It was a mess. Stacks of sealed cardboard boxes lined walls to the right and left.

Some stood against the back wall below a small curtained window.

I tried the light switch. It worked. I could see that the cat had clawed some of the boxes open. Maybe something inside them smelled good.

Tyler crossed the closet, being careful not to step on anything, and lifted the curtain. The window had four panes, and one of the top ones had broken.

"Guess the cat got in this way," he said.

"Treasure!" Alex shrieked, running into the closet and pouncing on something on the floor.

"Hey!" I cried. This closet was *off limits*. There was even a sign that said so! And we were definitely *not* supposed to go through other people's stuff when we stayed in their houses.

And Mom and Dad would be back any minute now, so...

I sat down with a thump. Time to go through some boxes!

Alex held up a little golden ball with softened spikes sticking out all over it. "Treasure!" he said again.

He was right. Everything in this room was totally cool-looking! Intricate, detailed, strange, and most of it was metallic.

I picked up a small oval pink thing with blue spots on it. I turned it over to find three little studs poking out. What was it? A piece from some game I'd never heard of? It was nice and heavy and solid. It would make a great pin for my denim jacket.

Tyler dropped down beside me. He reached for a palm-sized diamond-shaped silver thing with a rounded edge and raised brass studs on it. It looked like it was a remote control for something.

"Who are the people who live in this house?" Tyler asked. "And where did they get all this cool stuff?"

"I don't know, but we'd better put it all away," I said. Even though I *so totally* wanted to keep everything.

"Yeah," Tyler muttered. He picked up a tiny disk that looked like a Frisbee. It was metallic green with purple stripes on it. "Hey, it's just like on that doll," he said. He tipped it to show me.

Sure enough—there was a little black spot on the rim of the disk. Tyler tapped the black spot with one finger.

The Frisbee doubled in size.

Holy cow! I thought.

I grabbed six of the little metal things on the floor. Each was different from the others. But all of them had black pads on them!

Tyler grew the Frisbee two more times.

I glanced at Alex, who rolled the golden spiked ball and laughed as it zigzagged across the floor. "You'd better put that down," I told Tyler.

"But it's perfect for our movie," Tyler protested. "Special-effects city!"

He pulled his arm back as if he were going to throw the Frisbee.

"Stop that! You don't know what it's for!" I yelled. "Just shrink it, *right now!*"

"But it's *soooo* cool."

I glared at him. He sighed and tapped the black dot with two fingers, and the Frisbee shrank.

"Hide that somewhere Alex will never find it," I muttered to Tyler. He nodded and slipped the disk into his pocket.

"And we better check out the rest of this stuff later," I said. "Sometime when A-L-E-X is S-L-E-E-P-I-N-G."

Again, my brother nodded. We grabbed as many things off the floor as we could, righted a knocked-over box, and dumped everything into it.

Alex cried when we took the golden ball from him, but I packed it anyway. We put all the stuff away and had just relocked the closet door when I heard Mom and Dad jogging across the front porch.

"Whew," Tyler breathed, dropping the keys in his pocket.

"Yeah," I agreed. "That was a close one. If Mom and Dad caught us in there we'd be grounded for eternity!"

We spent the rest of the day doing family stuff. Mom and Dad took us on a picnic by the Pleasant Valley River, and we checked out a mall on the edge of town that had a fourplex at it. Then we went roller-skating.

A couple of times I managed to forget about all the weird things in our new house and have fun.

It wasn't until Mom and Dad went out for a romantic dinner that Tyler and I finally had a chance to do some more exploring. Well, first we had to feed Alex and get him to bed. We didn't want him tagging along.

Thankfully, he's a good sleeper, so he was out like a light in minutes.

We went to my room and got the doll down. Then we checked out all the other dolls. Not one of them had a black patch like the boy.

Tyler flicked a glance at me, then tapped the patch on the back of the boy doll's neck.

"Wait! We have to make sure he can't do anything when he wakes up." I pointed to my bruised wrist to prove my point.

"How?" Tyler asked. He tapped the black patch, and the doll grew to Alex's size.

"Maybe we could tie him up or something."

I looked around the room, searching for ideas. I frowned at the quilt on my bed. "I've got it!" I cheered.

I ran downstairs to the back porch where Dad had stowed some of the stuff we brought with us from California. I grabbed three long, stretchy bungee cords and headed upstairs again.

"Let's roll him in the quilt—except for his head. Then we can hook the bungee cords around him," I said. "That way no matter what size he is, he'll be tied up tight."

Tyler thought about it. "Okay. Sounds like it should work."

We wrapped the quilt around him pretty loosely. The bungee cords fit without stretching.

Tyler glanced at me. I nodded.

He tapped the patch on the back of the boy doll's neck.

The boy doll grew, filling out the quilt. The cords tightened around his arms, waist, and legs.

The doll blinked three times. "Huh?" he said, swiveling his head to look down at his trapped body.

Tyler and I studied him. He squirmed around, but it looked like he couldn't get loose.

Even better, we could still get to the patch on his neck and shrink him if we wanted, and he couldn't stop us.

"Hey!" he said, sounding panicked. "You guys woke me up before! Why—who are you?"

"Our turn to ask the questions," Tyler said. "Tell us who *you* are first."

"Me?" He gulped. "I, uh, I'm Brad Mills."

"Okay," I said. "*What* are you?"

"Huh?" He looked totally confused.

"What *are* you?"

"I'm a, well, a kid," he said.

"A couple minutes ago you were a doll," Tyler pointed out.

"I was?" Brad blinked three more times. "That's right. I guess I was."

"How do you explain that?" Tyler demanded.

"How do I explain it?" Brad muttered as if talking to himself. "I don't know…it's kind of hard. And the details are a little fuzzy from all the shrinking and unshrinking…" He paused. "But there's one thing I *do* remember…aliens did it to me! *Aliens!* And they could do it to you, too!"

CHAPTER 6

Aliens turned people into dolls? No way!

The best horror movies showed aliens doing lots of awful things to people. *Those* were the movies that gave me my worst nightmares. But turning people into toys? That didn't make any sense.

"Wait," I started. "Why would aliens want to shrink you into a doll?"

"They have this machine that shrinks you and puts a black touch pad on you," the doll answered. "Bing! They can shrink and grow you as much as they want."

"Okay. We'll buy the idea of a shrinking machine. But you haven't answered our question," Tyler pointed out. "*Why* would they do it?"

Brad closed his eyes. When he opened them, he looked sad and scared. "It makes you easier to transport," he answered.

"Huh?" Tyler and I asked at the same time.

"You make kids small, you can stack them pretty deep in a cargo hold. Once you fill your cargo hold with hundreds of kids, then you can go off trading."

"Trading?" I whispered. "Trading for what?"

"Anything you want. Human children are in high demand all over the galaxy. At least, that's what the aliens told me."

I raised an eyebrow. "What's so special about human kids?" I asked.

"Their taste." Brad shuddered. "According to the aliens, all the best space restaurants have human kids on the menu."

A chill prickled through me.

"It's like those restaurants you go to where you can pick your own live lobster," Brad went on.

"They have shelves of dolls, and people can select the one they want to snack on. The waiters take the dolls to the kitchen and...well, you get the picture."

For a second I felt dizzy. This story was too horrible to be true! Then again, last week I would have thought growing talking dolls were too weird to be true, too.

"So." Tyler narrowed his eyes. "So why are you on somebody's shelf instead of a plate in an alien restaurant somewhere?"

"I don't know," Brad mused. "The last thing I remember is some alien shrinking me. I just knew I was going to be eaten the next time I woke up." He squirmed around. "Instead, I'm here. Tied up. They must have accidentally left me behind or something."

He paused, thinking. Then he let out a gasp. "I just remembered something! The programming—the device!"

"What are you talking about?" I asked.

"The aliens brainwashed me. They programmed me to signal them in case I escaped," the doll-boy said. "Did I do anything strange the first time you tapped me up?"

"You reached under my bed for something," I remembered.

The doll-boy glanced at the bed. "Oh, no," he moaned. "It's too late. I've already activated the device."

"What device?" I asked.

"It's under the bed," the doll-boy told us.

Tyler knelt down and flipped up the bedspread.

"What's that?" he yelped. A pink pulsing light spread out from under my mattress. I noticed that faint dentist-drill whine again. I guessed it had been going on all along, and the quilt muffled the sound. I stooped and peered under my bed just as Tyler reached for something. It was a little pink glowing pyramid.

"It's a beacon to call the aliens to Blairingville. They programmed me to activate it. Now they're following it to this house!" The doll-boy struggled against the bungee cords.

I kneeled beside the bed. I peered at the pink pyramid. Light flashed from it in irregular waves.

"How long has it been broadcasting? *How long ago did you make me big?*" the doll-boy asked.

"It was last night," I answered.

"What time is it now?" He turned his head and looked at the bedside clock. "Nine-fifteen!" he cried. "Oh, no!"

"What?" Tyler demanded.

"You've *got* to let me go," Brad told us in a low, tense voice. He strained against the bungee cords. "If that beacon has been broadcasting for almost twenty-four hours, the aliens will be here any minute. You have to untie me! We have to hide!"

I wasn't sure that I should trust this guy. I mean, what if he was lying? What if he was just trying to get us to let him go?

I didn't have to wait long for my answer.

A low thrumming noise sounded from outside the house. It thumped the floor under me. Shaking it.

Tyler ran to the window, lifted the curtain, and peered outside. "Randi," he choked. Lavender and red light pulsed against his face.

I raced to join him. And gasped in shock.

In the backyard next door, glowing with purple and red lights, a large, saucer-shaped ship hovered above the ground.

CHAPTER 7

"They're here!" Brad cried, thrashing around. "They're here! We have to hide! Hurry!"

Tyler and I glanced at each other. Tyler dropped the curtain. We ran to Brad and unhooked the bungee cords around him. Brad struggled out of the quilt, then gripped Tyler's shoulders and mine. "We have get away from them! Do you understand?" The look in his eyes was totally intense.

I felt sweat trickle down my neck.

"Where is a good place to hide?" Brad demanded.

I panicked. We hadn't spent much time exploring the house. We had no idea where to hide—especially from aliens.

Then it hit me. "The off-limits closet," I said.

"I still have the key ring," Tyler told us, patting his pocket.

I grabbed Alex, who was sleepy and whiny, from his crib.

Tyler got the closet unlocked, and we all piled into it. Brad backed into one of the boxes we had opened earlier. It fell over, and some of those weird little things inside scattered on the floor.

"What the—?" Brad stooped down, his hands darting among glittering objects.

I grabbed stuff, too. We had to stop making noise!

Tyler pulled the door shut and was trying to get the key into the lock from the inside. "This isn't going to work," he rasped. "We can't lock it from the inside."

"Maybe if we're all really quiet," I began.

"No," Brad snapped. "If they can get in…"

"Waaaaaaaaah!" Alex bellowed.

"Quiet!" I whispered at him, putting my hand over his mouth.

Alex continued sniffling and sobbing, but very softly.

Brad gripped my arm. "We need a better place to hide."

"I know," I whispered. I wished I could think of something!

We sneaked out of the closet, and Tyler locked it again. We headed for the staircase. Maybe if we could get downstairs fast enough, we could rush outside.

But purple lights flashed through the first floor of the house. We heard little scrabbling noises from below us. They sounded like sticks scraping on wood. The air reeked of ammonia.

We couldn't see them, but we knew. The aliens— the *kid-eating* aliens—were already downstairs.

CHAPTER 8

"There's a huge tree out my bedroom window," Tyler whispered. "It's got a branch that we can climb out on. Let's go!"

We sneaked into Tyler's bedroom and eased the door shut. Brad ran to the window, opened the curtains, and inched the glass pane up.

There *was* a giant tree out there, but it looked pretty far away. Also, it was so dark. I couldn't see the tree very well. My entire body quaked with fear.

Brad got on his knees on the windowsill. He lunged across to the tree and landed on the big limb—no problem. He inched along the limb away from us.

"Hey!" Tyler whispered. "Help us with Alex!"

Brad edged back along the limb and held out his arms.

"Don't wanna, don't wanna," Alex muttered.

Tyler climbed on the windowsill, then turned and held out his hands. I gave Alex to him, then grabbed the back of his pants. I didn't want him falling out the window as he handed Alex over to Brad. "Be careful," I pleaded.

Brad took Alex and slid toward the tree trunk again. Then he climbed down a couple branches, leaving the big branch free.

Then Tyler crouched on the windowsill. He leaped across to the branch. *Oof!* He landed on his stomach. His face paled, but he held on while the branch dipped up and down. He edged along the branch to leave me some room.

I climbed up on the window ledge. More scrabbles and clicks sounded from downstairs.

The aliens! It was now or never.

I leaned out—jumped for the branch. And missed!

I grabbed frantically and managed to catch hold of it. The rough bark scratched my hands. I wasn't going to be able to hold on for long!

"Come on, Randi," Tyler whispered from above, touching my hand. "Arm over arm."

I remembered the playground equipment I loved to use as a kid. I was a pro on the monkey bars.

I made my way into the tree's big canopy. Brad guided my feet to a lower branch.

I leaned against the tree, sagging with relief.

"We can't stay here," Brad murmured.

He was right. I could see the backyard, and the spaceship that had landed in it. It looked like the top and bottom of a merry-go-round squashed together without the horses in between. A ramp stretched out from the bottom. These...*things* ran down the ramp.

They looked like pony-sized lizards—like the velociraptors in that cool dinosaur movie. Except that they had long, purple, curved tales with rattle things on the end.

And two huge fangs poking out of their mouths like a snake.

They were huge space reptiles—with legs!

"We've got to get out of here," Brad whispered.

The space reptiles ran between the spaceship and the back door. They didn't seem interested in the side of the house, so we were in the clear—for now.

Brad climbed down a few branches and dropped to the ground. He held up his arms so we could lower Alex into them.

I was scared and limp and tired, but I made my arms and legs work. I climbed down out of the tree. Tyler followed.

A loud chittering noise sounded from the house.

I glanced over and saw one of those awful reptile heads peering out of the living room window!

No! I thought. It can't see me! I froze in my tracks.

The reptile made screechy noises, like cars crashing into each other, metal denting other metal.

Two more heads poked out of the window beside the first one. No! They knew we were here!

Tyler grabbed my arm. "Come on! Run!"

I stumbled toward the street, but deep down I knew there was no way we could outrun them all!

The four of us were toast!

CHAPTER 9

"Run!" Brad yelled. He shoved Alex into my arms. My baby brother tightened his grip around my neck as I ran.

The chittering and screeching noises closed in on us. What if I tripped? Would they eat us right here?

No. I couldn't trip, I *wouldn't*, I told myself.

We put on a burst of speed. Tyler ran beside me. Brad pulled on ahead. I heard the aliens' reptile feet scrabbling on the sidewalk. The sound was getting louder. They were closing in!

Brad reached the end of the block and stopped under the street light.

Something hard stepped on my heel, nearly jerked my shoe off. The sharp smell of ammonia invaded my nostrils.

Terror shot through me. The space reptiles were right behind us!

Tyler grabbed my shoulder and pushed me. I ran faster than I ever had before.

We stumbled into the circle of light the street-light cast on the sidewalk. Brad snagged my arm as I tried to dash past him.

"What are you doing?" I managed to huff.

He pointed behind me, slowing down.

The space reptiles were running away!

"They're not disguised," Brad explained. "So they can't stick around long, and they can't risk being noticed by anyone. If we go anywhere people can see us, they'll have to leave us alone!"

"Let's go to the mall," Tyler suggested. "It's Saturday night. There are probably tons of people there!"

We checked for aliens in the street. The coast was clear. We ran and ran, from the light of one street-lamp to another.

At last we reached our destination. I was never so happy to see a mall in my life! We pushed inside and headed straight to the video arcade, where local kids were playing way outdated games. I didn't know any of those kids, but right then I loved them all.

Tyler ran over to the Addams Family pinball machine. It was one of his favorites. I sat down on the chair of a racetrack simulator nobody was using, and placed Alex in my lap.

"They'll never follow us here," Brad said. He smiled at all the flashing screens. Messages blinked across them:

FIGHT ALIEN INVADERS! SAVE THE PLANET!

Yeah, right. Let someone else fight the aliens, I thought.

"We can't hang out here all night," I muttered. I shifted Alex in my lap. He was heavy and sleepy now.

"We won't have to," Brad reassured us. "They can't stay at your house long. They didn't come prepared for a stealth mission. When they want to stay a while, they use human bodies."

"Use human bodies?" I asked. "Hold on. You mean besides eating humans, they *take over* their bodies?"

"Yup. They make replica bodies and switch their thoughts into them," Brad told us in a matter-of-fact tone.

"Wow." I heaved a sigh. "It's so much to try to understand at once."

Brad's face softened. "Yeah. I guess it must be. I've been living with it longer, so it makes more sense to me." He smiled. "Just relax. You'll be okay now."

He strutted over to the pinball machine where Tyler was. The two began playing.

I leaned back in the chair of the racing game and closed my eyes. I was pooped.

Then I glanced outside the arcade into the mall. It was so reassuring. People—normal people—wandered around, shopping.

Normal people…like Mom and Dad.

Wait, wasn't that—yes! Mom and Dad walking by the arcade! We'd be safe with them!

I tightened my grip on Alex and ran into the mall. "Mom! Dad!" I called. They turned and stared at me, shocked expressions on both of their faces.

"Randi! What are you doing here?" Mom asked.

Alex woke up and looked around. "Mama?" he said. I let him down and he ran to her. "Mama!" He hugged her around the knees.

"What is going on here?" Dad demanded. "Randi, who gave you permission to leave the house at night?"

Mom leaned over, detached Alex from her legs, and swung him up into her arms.

"I—" I tried again. I was never going to be able to explain this, I realized. Not unless Mom and Dad came home and saw the aliens for themselves.

And I wanted them to! I wanted them to call the police or the FBI or whoever was supposed to deal with alien invaders!

On the other hand, I never wanted to go back to that house again!

"Blairingville seems safe enough," Dad went on, "but I still don't want you wandering around in a strange place at night."

Safe? Blairingville wasn't safe! Our own *house* wasn't safe.

"I—" I said again.

"What's gotten into you?" Dad persisted.

"Big lizard at the house," Alex babbled. "We climbed out a window and jumped on a tree. I almost failed."

"What?" Mom asked, her voice faint.

"Lizard, big lizard!" Alex yelled. "It stinked!"

"Randi!" Dad said. "Have you been letting Alex watch horror movies again? You *know* he gets nightmares!"

"No! I—"

"You are grounded, Randi! You are grounded for the rest of this vacation!" Dad yelled.

"But— " I began.

Tyler came dashing out of the arcade with Brad behind him. "Mom! Dad! Am I glad to see you!"

Tyler cried, and he rushed over and hugged Mom. She should have known right then that something was wrong. Tyler never hugged unless he was ordered to.

"Tyler," Dad said in a low, serious voice. "Did you let Alex watch horror movies?"

"Huh?" Tyler asked. "What do you—"

"Well, you're grounded, too, young man," Dad interrupted.

I tugged on his sleeve. "Dad, you have to listen. We weren't watching horror movies. Alex is right. There were giant reptile creatures at the house."

"What?" Dad demanded.

"There were. Tell him there were, Tyler! Tell him!"

Brad whispered something in Tyler's ear. Tyler laughed.

Huh? Giant fanged lizards from space almost caught and barbecued us, and my twin brother was laughing?

How *could* he?

"Randi fell asleep while we were watching this movie," Tyler said. His voice was really strange. It sounded—detached. Distracted. "She dreamed the whole thing. We didn't climb out the window. We walked over here."

"That's not true!" I cried.

"Grounded!" Dad yelled back. "Both of you!"

Dad never grounds us for anything. I felt horrible. Then I thought: being grounded means we have to stay in that house.

"We didn't know we were doing anything wrong," Tyler continued in his weird voice. "Mom, Dad, this is Brad Mills. He lives here in town. He said he'd watch out for us, show us where the other kids spend their Saturday nights."

"You *know* you're not supposed to leave the house without permission," Dad said, but his voice calmed down a little.

"Hi, Brad," Mom said. "Larry, aren't you glad the kids are making *friends* here." She shot Dad a look.

He thought for a couple minutes. He sighed. "Okay, you guys. This is your first offense for this trip. I won't ground you for it. But from now on, no leaving the house at night without permission from me or Mom, got it?"

"But, Dad—" I insisted.

Dad frowned deeply at me. "Randi!"

"We understand, Dad," Tyler said in a rush. "Say, can Brad spend the night tonight?"

"We'll check with his parents," Mom offered.

Brad smiled that perfect smile at her. "Thanks, Mrs. Freeman," he said. She smiled back.

"Well, we were about to head back and check on you," Dad said. "I think it's time we all went home."

"Sure, Dad." Tyler grinned.

What was wrong with my brother? "But what about—" I began. What if the space lizards were still there?

I swallowed the rest of my sentence. If the aliens *were* still there, Mom and Dad would call the police. That would be okay by me—as long as the aliens didn't see us.

We made it home okay in the station wagon. No aliens came after us. But when Dad parked in the driveway, I didn't want to get out of the car. What if there were still aliens in the house?

Dad stared at the front door. It gaped open. Light from inside spilled across the porch.

"Did you kids leave that door open?" Dad demanded, glaring over the seat at us.

"No!" Tyler and I cried at the same time. We hadn't used the front door all evening. Just an upstairs window.

"Wait here," Dad ordered all of us.

"But shouldn't we call the police?" I asked.

"It's okay. I'm just going to check this out," Dad murmured. He got out of the car and crossed the lawn, peering at the house.

But—what if the aliens were waiting for him? I leaned forward to yell to Dad to come back, but Brad, beside me in the backseat, put his hand over my mouth. "Don't worry," he whispered so Mom couldn't hear from the front seat. "They're gone."

I nodded, but how could he be so sure?

Dad crossed the porch to the front door. He stood there for a moment and called into the house—I couldn't hear what he said.

Then he stepped over the threshold and vanished inside.

Minutes ticked by. No Dad. No sound. Nothing from inside the house. What was happening in there? Why wasn't he coming out?

A horrible thought crossed my mind.

Did the aliens get him?

CHAPTER 10

"I'm not waiting any longer," Mom said after another five minutes had passed. "Let's go, kids." She opened the car door and strode toward the house.

"Wait! Mom! We should call the police," I called, climbing out after her. I glanced around the neighborhood. "We could ask the neighbors to call," I said, pointing to an occupied house down the street.

Mom thought about it for a minute. "First we'll go to the door and yell. Maybe your father just got distracted."

We climbed up on the porch, and Mom stuck her head into the house. "What stinks in here? Were you kids doing science experiments in the kitchen again?" she cried.

"No," I said.

"Yes," Tyler answered at the same time.

What was *with* him? I turned to glare at him.

He and Brad stood close together, close enough for Brad to whisper to him. Tyler tapped his index finger with his other index finger, which, in our twin code, meant *Follow me on this.*

I whirled my finger by my head. *Are you crazy?*

"Larry?" Mom called. "Larry, are you all right? If you don't answer me, I'm calling the police!"

"I'm fine, Helen. Everything's fine!" Dad yelled from upstairs. "What made this horrible mess?"

Mess? I thought back. We straightened up the off-limits closet, didn't we? I thought we relocked it, too. I couldn't remember. Everything was all jumbled in my head.

Mom, Tyler, and Brad went inside. I followed slightly behind, still scouting for stray aliens.

"Whoa," Tyler gasped from the top of the stairs.

I bumped into him. He stared into my bedroom. It looked as though a whirlwind had hit it. All the furniture had shifted. The bedspread, blankets, and sheets had been torn off the bed, and everything had been knocked off the dresser. The dresser drawers were pulled out and emptied onto the floor.

All the dolls had come off the shelves. They were scattered across the floor—and so was everything from the closet.

Over it all, that horrible ammonia stink still hung in the air, even though the window was wide open.

I felt like somebody had punched me in the stomach.

I glanced at Tyler. I wondered if he felt as creeped out and mad as I did. Sometimes we had the same feelings at the same time.

Tyler just stared ahead blankly.

Mom stood right behind me and put her warm hands on my shoulders. "Oh, honey," she said. "It looks like we've been robbed."

No! I wanted to shout. *That's not it at all!*

"We've got to call the police," Dad said.

He trooped downstairs to the phone. Tyler and Brad waded through dolls and debris to the window, and I followed them. We looked out into the backyard.

The lawn sat there, empty again. No lights, no spaceship, no giant space lizards dashing around.

After a moment I felt relieved. I let out a huge sigh. At least the aliens really *were* gone.

"Yes!" Brad said, pounding his right fist into his left palm. "They've given up! Awesome!" He thumped Tyler's shoulder, then mine. I had to smile at him, he seemed so happy.

Of course he is, I thought. He's free from the aliens now.

A police officer came by the house fifteen minutes later and looked around. He asked me if anything was missing. I told him I couldn't tell in all this mess, but I didn't think so.

He checked through the rest of the house, with all of us following. Everything looked perfectly normal except my room.

The officer told Dad he'd file a report on breaking and entering and malicious mischief, and he'd get back to us if he found out anything about it. He apologized that we out-of-town visitors had to have this "upsetting experience."

Upsetting experience! I wanted to laugh. He had no idea how upsetting my experience had been!

Mom and Dad helped me clean everything up.

One of the dolls had cracked her porcelain face. We collected all the pieces on a plate. Mom said that maybe we could glue her back together.

Other dolls had dirty clothes or messy hair. We set aside all the ones that needed the most work and put the rest back on the shelves in as close to their old order as I could remember.

I still hate dolls, but I also hated the thought of that girl coming home and seeing her stuff so messed up.

By the time we'd finished, it was really late. I felt totally exhausted.

Most of the stink was gone from my room, but I still didn't want to sleep there. So mom said I could sleep on the couch.

She had to throw Tyler and Brad out of the living room, though. They were lounging around, eating microwave popcorn and watching horror movies.

How could they be hanging out, acting as if nothing had happened, when we had just been through the most terrifying experience of our lives? It was totally weird. I couldn't understand it. I was so exhausted that I couldn't wait to hit the sack.

I yawned—and decided to ask Tyler about it tomorrow.

When I opened my eyes the next morning, Tyler, Brad, and Alex were sitting way close to the TV. They slurped cereal out of bowls.

At least, Tyler and Alex were slurping cereal. Brad just lifted spoonfuls and dropped them back into the bowl. Again, totally weird.

"Yow! What a night!" I said. "Is everyone okay?"

Brad turned around and smiled at me. "Everything's great. They're gone for good now."

Tyler gulped down a mouthful of cereal. "Wasn't that totally cool? Weren't those space reptiles perfect for our movie? Brad and I have been figuring out how to make costumes that look just like them."

"What? Are you *nuts*? I don't want those things anywhere *near* our movie!" I cried. "I never want to see them or anything like them ever again!"

"But they were really scary," Tyler argued. "Besides, our movie isn't *about* anything. We just keep filming cool stuff and hoping we can put it all together later.

"Brad and I have been talking about how to give our movie a *plot*," he continued. "If we figure out the story, Brad and I can just film the scenes we need and finally put it all together."

Brad and I? I thought. Whose movie was this, anyway? And since when did Tyler, my twin and my best friend, just abandon me?

I didn't like this. I didn't like it one bit.

"Brad thinks we should forget all the stuff about ghosts and just use aliens instead," Tyler told me, waving his spoon.

"But—" What about all our great tape of New Orleans cemeteries? Were we supposed to throw that out?

"But, Tyler—"

"We can open with a scene of all those dolls, once they get cleaned up," Tyler went on.

I glanced at Brad, who was smiling at Tyler. This was all his idea. I could tell. And for some reason, the whole situation made me uneasy. I wanted Brad gone from our lives—as soon as possible.

"So, Brad," I interrupted my brother, "now that the spaceship's gone, you can go home to your parents, right?"

"My...parents?" Brad hesitated, as though he never heard of parents before.

"Sure. You grew up here in Blairingville, right? So I guess we should phone your family. In fact, we should phone them right away," I pressed on.

"Uhhh—what year is it?" Brad asked slowly.

I told him.

"Oh, man. I've been a doll for two years," he explained. "My parents must think I'm dead! There's no way I can call them now."

I raised an eyebrow. "But—don't you want to see them again?"

He blinked. "I need to figure out how to tell them I'm still alive so they won't die of heart attacks when they see me. I just need a little time."

Wow. That made no sense at *all*. I couldn't imagine not letting my parents know that I was okay—especially if I'd been missing for two years. Unless I'd gone crazy or something.

Wait a minute…maybe that was it. Maybe Brad was nuts. I mean, who knew what being shrunk down to dollsize by giant lizards would do to a person.

"I'm just sooo glad to be able to move again," Brad said. He held his hand up in front of his face and moved his fingers one at a time, then all together.

I watched him intently as he continued to talk to Tyler about what would make a great horror movie. I caught a strange gleam in his eye. One that made me shudder. No doubt. Brad was off his rocker. He couldn't stay.

And if I wanted to get rid of him, I knew I'd have to bring out my big guns.

I was going to have to talk to Mom.

CHAPTER 11

If I could just get Mom to ask Brad about his parents, I was home free. She wouldn't give up. She would *make* Brad call them. I was surprised she hadn't insisted he call them last night. I guess all the confusion threw her Mom instincts off or something.

Before I put Plan "Mom Attacks!" into operation, I took a shower. When I reached the kitchen afterward, everyone was sitting around the table.

I grabbed the box of Chocolate Puffs and poured a bowlful.

"So, like I was saying," Tyler told us, "there was an emergency with Brad's uncle in Mexico. His family had to leave town. They couldn't wait for Brad to join them. So—can he stay with us?"

What? This was a totally different story from the one Brad told earlier! And it was *way* lame! The guy *was* wacko if he thought my parents were going to fall for this!

Looks like Brad just saved me the trouble of putting Plan "Mom Attacks!" into action. I chuckled to myself.

I munched my cereal, waiting for Mom to kick into high gear.

Brad sat back in his chair, playing with a pendant he had hanging on a black string around his neck. I hadn't noticed it before. A pink jewel on it flashed in the light from the overhead fixture.

I glanced at Mom. She would blast this story to bits in two seconds.

But instead, she just sat there, her mouth half open, staring at Brad.

Tiny squares and diamonds of light danced across her face, glinted from her eyes. I turned to Dad. Light glittered across his face, too.

Out of the corner of my eye I saw Brad shift the pendant. That's where the light was coming from! Brad was aiming the light reflected through his pendant right at my parents. But why?

Mom's mouth snapped shut. "Of course," she said after a minute. "We'd *love* to have Brad stay with us as long as he likes."

"Whaaaaaat?" I yelled.

"Would you like some more breakfast, Brad?" Mom asked, ignoring my outburst.

"No, thanks, Mrs. Freeman," he replied, cupping his hand around the pendant and smiling his broad, white smile.

I looked at his plate. It was filled with eggs and toast. It didn't look as if he'd eaten anything—so why was Mom offering him more breakfast?

Something was wrong around here. Something *majorly* weird was happening!

I shook my head. No, this was more than weird. My parents weren't acting the way they should—the way I *knew* they normally would.

It seemed as if Brad was somehow influencing them. Controlling them so he could get his way. Was he using the pendant to do it?

No. That couldn't be. It was impossible. Wasn't it?

"Mom?" I started.

"Yes, dear?" Mom turned to me. Her eyes had a fuzzy-looking, confused expression in them. Not their usual clear-eyed, piercing stare.

Whoa. This was bad. I needed to think—and fast. "Nothing," I responded.

Tyler jumped up. "Let's go outside!" he called. Brad and Alex followed him.

I drank the rest of my Chocolate Puffs like soup and hurried after them.

Tyler knelt on the lawn, examining grass blades. "Did it leave any marks?" he muttered. *"AHA!"* He pounced on a patch of grass, burrowed through it. "Look!" He pointed to a large, deep depression in the dirt.

I squatted beside him and stared down. It was a triangular footprint created by the spaceship.

"We should call the FBI," Tyler said. "Better yet, we should call a TV station! We could be on TV!" He jumped up and ran to another place where grass looked torn up.

"Are you nuts?" I asked Tyler. "There's no way you could tell that this impression was left by a spaceship. Any kid with a sand shovel could dig a hole like this!"

I sat back on my heels and sighed as Tyler danced around another hole in the ground. Alex laughed and clapped his hands nearby.

I glanced at Brad, who knelt near me by the first hole. He was leaning forward on his hands, his head hanging. He wasn't smiling anymore. His face was gray and pale. I wondered if he was going to hurl.

I leaned forward. "Hey," I started.

He lifted his head and stared me in the face. His eyes looked sunken. A shudder went through him.

And then...

His face melted away.

Instead of Brad, I stared into the hideous face of a space lizard!

CHAPTER 12

A space lizard with thick, scaly purple skin, cold yellow eyes, and long sharp fangs.

I yelped and jumped back. My heart raced. Sweat popped out on my forehead.

Brad had *promised* us that all the aliens had left! But he'd lied. All the aliens had left—except *him*!

I swallowed hard, and blinked.

The lizard head vanished.

Brad smiled at me, looking like a toothpaste commercial again. Tan, not gray. Blond-haired, not purple and scaly. Straight white teeth, not fangs.

Whew! It was just a leftover nightmare.

I was just hallucinating! Right?

At that moment, I decided, I didn't care if I was hallucinating or not. I needed to get away from Brad.

I straightened, and Brad held up his pendant. Sunlight caught in the pink jewel. For a second it blinded me. I tried to shield my eyes, but I couldn't.

Don't move, a voice in my head said. I realized I couldn't move a muscle.

Sit down, the voice commanded. I plopped down on the grass.

You saw my true face. I know you did. You know that I'm one of them, the voice continued.

I saw Brad staring at me, and I realized that it was his voice—*Brad's* voice inside my head.

They returned to take me away. But I didn't want to go with them. Do you understand?

My head nodded at Brad.

Good, his voice sounded in my brain. *I just want to stay here. But to do that, I need some very special help from one of you.* His blue eyes widened. They looked fever-bright as they stared into mine.

"You're the one I need, Randi," he said out loud, lifting the pendant. "Alex is too small, your parents are too important to my future, and, well, I'm already bonding successfully with Tyler. I'm sorry, Randi. I like you, too. Just not as much as I like Tyler."

He flashed the crystal in my eyes again. I felt hypnotized by the patterns I saw in the light: snow-flakes and flowers, dazzling and beautiful.

"Listen carefully," Brad's voice whispered to me. "You *will* obey me. You can't say anything that will give me away, and you'll do whatever I tell you to, without question."

I blinked. The light felt like it was pricking me now, piercing my skin like shards of broken glass.

I tried to shake my head, but I couldn't.

I swallowed again.

"Lie down on the porch," he said.

I walked over to the porch and lay on my back.

"Now, sit up," Brad whispered.

I snapped upright so suddenly my stomach hurt.

Brad patted me on the head. Patted me! Like an obedient dog!

"Good," he said.

His face twisted into a strange grin.

No! This can't be happening, my mind screamed. This can't be happening, but it *is*!

I'm being controlled by an alien!

CHAPTER 13

Brad heaved a huge sigh and settled himself on the porch. "Good. Now that that's settled…" He patted the bench beside him. "Sit here."

I jerked up like a puppet on strings and flopped down next to him. My skin twitched. I couldn't believe it. It was as if I had no control over my body at all. Brad told me to sit next to him. So I did. *Right* next to him. I could not shift even a couple of inches away.

"Here's my problem," Brad continued. "This human body isn't a very good one. It was only meant to last as long as our mission on this planet—one year. But right near the end of our mission, we messed up. And we all got shrinked."

"Shrinked?" I said. Then I touched my throat, surprised that I could talk without his permission.

"Oh, you know." He patted the back of his neck, where that black touch spot was. I had forgotten about it. If only I had used it to shrink him before he started waving that pendant around!

"An Earthling used our own technology against us. That's why I ended up on your shelf," he continued.

I gulped. "So, wait a minute. All that stuff about aliens shrinking kids and eating them—you made that up, right? Those aliens weren't coming to eat us—they were coming to get you?"

"Yup." He shrugged. "But, as I was saying, this body is falling apart. It won't last much longer. I need to build a new one, a better one, one that can digest Earth food and sleep on Earth beds. One that will last for years."

He stared into the distance for a while. "We have another kind of technology that lets us switch bodies with other species, but that's not a long-term solution," he said. "I could jump into your body and put you into mine, but I would wear out your primitive anatomy in just another year. Your body would be useless. What I want is a more permanent answer."

I licked my lip and waited to hear his plan.

"Fortunately," he continued, "the ones who came for me missed all the equipment in that closet upstairs. So I have the technology to grow an entirely new body and switch my consciousness into it. But I need a human blueprint to help me shape it right, get all those little Earth details in place. I need to create the right kind of stomach and intestines, and hair that doesn't fall out, and a balance system that doesn't need to spend sleep time upside down. It would also be nice if my heart were in the right place, instead of down by my stomach."

He stared at my face a minute, then smiled sadly. "I could use Tyler as a blueprint, but Tyler's my friend. Randi, you'll have to do."

I felt cold all over. Brad was going to use me as a human blueprint? What did that mean? Whatever it was, it didn't sound good.

He grinned, one corner of his mouth higher than the other. "Don't worry," he whispered, patting my head again. "It won't hurt…much."

CHAPTER 14

I closed my eyes. Brad *was* planning to hurt me—maybe even kill me—and there was no way I could escape!

"Hey, Brad?" Tyler yelled, still running and jumping on the lawn.

Brad straightened. "Oh, yeah. I forgot." He leaned forward and flashed the pendant toward Tyler. "You can relax now," he whispered, and Tyler collapsed in a heap with Alex beside him, both of them tired from all that dancing around.

Brad got up, and I did, too.

Whew! I had told my body to move, I realized. And this time it had listened. Right now I was moving because I decided to.

Brad headed across the porch toward the lawn. Could I make a break for it? I wondered. No way, I realized. Brad could turn and command me at any second. He'd stop me dead in my tracks.

Brad walked one step below me down the steps. That black touch pad on his neck was right in front of me. I couldn't run, but maybe I could shrink him before he said anything. Then I could stop him from ever ordering me around again!

I reached out to touch the back of his neck.

He whirled and grabbed my hand. He squeezed so hard I could feel my bones grinding together. *"Never do that again!"* he said. His voice was fierce. His eyes so wide open I could see the whites all around the irises.

Still holding my hand tight, he raised the pendant in his other hand and flashed light at me. "If you *ever* try to harm me again, you'll feel like you're burning up! Burning to death!"

He gave my hand one last good squeeze and then let go.

I felt sick to my stomach. What was I supposed to do now? I was powerless against Brad. Absolutely powerless.

Brad strolled over to where Tyler was and sat down.

"I don't know," Tyler said, sitting up and peering at the torn-up place in the lawn. "I thought at first this was going to be big news, but you can't really tell anything from it."

He poked the hole in the dirt with his finger. "*I* know there was a spaceship here last night, but nobody would really believe it just looking at a stupid hole in the ground. I don't get why I was so excited about it. There's no *real* evidence of alien visitors here at all."

Look right in front of you if you want to see an alien visitor, I wanted to tell Tyler. I opened my mouth...

And started coughing and choking!

I coughed so hard I fell to the ground. I couldn't stop!

Brad looked down at me. "What's the matter?" He chuckled. "Alien in your throat?" Then he leaned closer and whispered, "I commanded you not to talk about it, remember? Try and you'll just hurt yourself."

I coughed so deep I felt like my lungs were coming up. All right, I thought. I will not talk about this to anyone.

I stopped coughing. But my throat burned and my ribs hurt from the fit I had. Oh, man! Brad could turn my body against me completely! How could I fight against that?

I sleepwalked through the rest of the morning, following Tyler as he checked through the house to see if the space lizards had left anything else behind. As he searched, my mind whirred. I had to figure some way out of this horrible mess!

After lunch Brad lifted his pendant again.

I flinched. What did he want *now*?

"Everyone but Randi, don't you feel like taking a nice nap?" Brad asked. "A nice *long* nap?"

"What a good idea," Dad said.

Mom yawned. Alex's eyes drifted shut.

"Go upstairs in your beds where you'll be comfortable," Brad commanded. "You'll have a restful sleep and, when I tell you to, you'll wake up feeling refreshed."

"Okay," Tyler said, blinking.

Mom, Dad, Tyler, and Alex all headed upstairs.

Brad smiled at me. "Okay!" he said cheerfully. "Now we can get to work."

He led the way upstairs. "Where's the key to the off-limits closet?" he asked.

I went and got it out of Tyler's room. Tyler lay on his back on the bed, fast asleep. He was so unconscious, he looked dead—even though I could hear him breathing.

Brad opened the closet, flicked on the light, and went directly to the boxes. He pawed through them all.

"Oh, yeah, perfect," he said in delighted tones, picking up several multicolored gadgets. "This is terrific! All I need now is to figure out where to set up my workshop."

He ran from the closet and peered out the windows in Mom and Dad's room. I followed him. "Is that house next door empty?" he asked.

"Yeah," I answered.

"Excellent. Come on."

We went back to the closet. Brad had me hold out my arms. Then he loaded me down with two boxes. He grabbed the third box himself.

I followed him around the back of the house next door. Brad took something out of his pocket and touched the back door with it. The door unlocked itself and opened.

"How did you do that?" I demanded.

"Universal key. It unlocks anything." Brad held up the gadget. "Life is going to be *so* good when I get my permanent body."

I could tell Brad was going to need his "permanent body" soon. His skin seemed to be getting loose and baggy. And kind of gray.

Ugh. Extremely gross, I thought.

Brad crossed the empty kitchen and opened a door. Behind it was a flight of stairs leading down to the basement. He flicked a light switch at the top of the stairs. It didn't work.

"Guess I'll have to supply my own power," he muttered. He set his box down and took another gadget out of his pocket. He tapped it bigger and switched it on. A globe of bright greenish light shone from it.

Wow. This alien stuff is totally amazing, I thought. He set the glowing lamp on his head and trotted down the stairs.

"Come on," he called. Carrying my two boxes, I followed behind.

The basement stood empty and cold. It smelled like mildew and decay. Brad held his light globe up on the low ceiling and it stuck there.

My eyes took in the basement scene. I could see a dark concrete floor with dust and grease on it. Some of the walls showed exposed two-by-fours and insulation. A huge square furnace stood in a dark corner, and shelves sectioned off another part of the basement.

Brad went to a skinny window and opened it with the universal key. Then he took tiny things out of the boxes and made them bigger. "Air filter," he said, setting up a weird wire pyramid in one corner.

"Power pack," he explained, taking another gadget over near the window. He enlarged it, and it grew to the size of a dishwasher. Brad pulled three yellow cords out of it.

"Grow tank," he muttered, tapping on something else laying on its side. It grew to shoebox size, then trunk size, then refrigerator size or maybe a little bigger.

I moved closer to check it out. I could see through the sides of it—see the shiny wiring laced inside of it. I shuddered. It was kind of like a strange, see-through coffin.

"And—" Brad tapped up a giant pink chair. Dangling from the chair's back was a drooping powder-blue flower-shaped thing as big as a large pizza.

Brad smiled at me. Not in a nice way.

He grabbed cords from the power pack and hooked them into the chair and the tank.

He pulled a fat, stretchy pink cord from the back of the chair and hooked it into something on the end of the grow tank.

Then he glanced my way and lifted an eyebrow.

"Have a seat," he said.

I tried to resist, tried to run back up the stairs and out of that house. But it was no use. Brad was in control.

I whimpered and walked over to the chair. I climbed up into it.

Brad tapped a bunch of colored buttons on the chair. Eight tentacles whipped out from the sides of the chair and wrapped around me, locking my arms and legs down and circling my waist.

The blue flower at the top of the chair's headrest lowered to touch my head. Its petals—cool, smooth, almost damp—draped over my face and hair. I felt their edges reach down to cover my neck.

Then the petals tightened—smothering me!

I couldn't see. I could barely breathe. And I could not move!

I gripped the ends of the chair arms, struggling to stay alive.

"Relax," Brad coached.

Again, I had to obey him. I relaxed. Completely. After a couple minutes I realized I could breathe just fine.

"Good," Brad said. Moments later the flower lifted off my face, and the chair's tentacles released me.

"We're all set," he said, "except for the shopping list. Let's go back to your house."

I followed him back. Of course.

Brad took Mom's magnetic grocery notepad from the refrigerator and grabbed a pencil. We sat at the kitchen table. Brad thought for a minute, wrote something.

Then he scratched his head with the point of the pencil.

I gasped in horror, watching him as—*Splat!* A huge clump of his hair and scalp fell to the table.

CHAPTER 15

I felt something sour rising in the back of my throat. A piece of Brad's head lay on the kitchen table.

His body was literally falling to pieces! I realized.

"Uuuugh," I moaned before I could stop myself. I slapped my hand over my mouth to keep myself from throwing up.

Brad glared at me with narrowed eyes.

"I guess we'll have to work faster than I thought," he muttered. He picked up the piece of scalp and tossed it in the garbage pail. I squeezed my eyes shut. Bile rose in my throat again. I swallowed hard.

"I'll need cell samples from everyone in your family," Brad continued, "so I can put together a basic gene map and..." He stopped and glanced up at me. "Never mind. Go do something for half an hour. I'll find you later."

I took a shower and changed my clothes. I had just finished drying my hair when Brad walked into my room.

"I loaded your family's cell samples into the grow tank while you were changing," Brad said. "Now there are a few other things we'll need." He took out a pad and paper and began scribbling a shopping list.

"Lots and lots of ground beef. Springwater, fourteen liters. Nothing but the best for my body. Trace elements. Where can I get cobalt, copper, iodine, manganese, and zinc?"

"Vitamins?" I suggested.

He made a note. "Vitamins. And twelve pounds of bananas," he muttered. Then he crossed the hall to my parents' room. He grabbed Mom's wallet.

"There's not enough cash here," he reported. He fished out my mom's debit card. "Do you know the PIN number for this?"

"What?" I felt totally outraged. How could he steal money from Mom without even thinking twice?

"I don't know Mom's number," I lied.

Brad frowned. "I'll figure something out," he said. He fished my mom's car keys out of her bag.

"You can't drive our car!" I yelled. "No. No way!"

A couple of minutes later we were driving to the supermarket.

Brad made a left turn. As he did, a strip of skin peeled off his forearm. It hung down, looking ugly, brown, rotten.

I stared at it. Nausea welled up in my stomach again.

"Nuts," he said, noticing his arm.

He pressed the skin back against the raw spot. It stuck. Sort of.

"I need a better shirt," he said. He glanced at mine. I was just wearing a tank top.

I crawled into the back of the station wagon and rummaged around until I came up with a paint-splashed work shirt of Dad's. At least it had long sleeves.

Brad grunted and put it on.

In the air-conditioned store he stuck Mom's debit card in the ATM and did something with his universal key. Twenty seconds later the machine spat a bunch of money at him.

We went shopping.

We had to use two carts. And we had to make several trips.

He bought eighty pounds of ground meat in those Family Packs that they have, and stew meat, too. He even got some bones from the butcher. Looking at all that red meat, thinking about what Brad wanted to do with it, well, it didn't help my nausea.

Dozens of eggs. Twelve pounds of bananas. Sixteen bottles of vitamins, cartons and cartons of salt. And so many gallon jugs of mountain spring water my arms wanted to fall out by the time we'd loaded them into the car.

After we left the supermarket, we went to a nursery. Brad bought a bunch of fertilizer, which really stunk up the car.

Then we went back to the vacant house. He made me carry the supplies down to the basement all by myself.

Brad opened the top of the grow tank and started dumping all that stuff in.

For a while I felt like we were throwing together a really weird protein drink.

When we'd completely loaded up the tank and he had locked down the lid, he said, "Now for the fun part. Go sit in that chair again."

I'd tried the chair before, and it hadn't been so bad, I told myself. I sighed and climbed into it. Brad made it wrap me up in tentacles and flower petals again, and I leaned back and relaxed. Yes. Now that I wasn't afraid of the chair anymore, it actually *was* comfortable.

But then Brad turned it on.

For real.

A horrible surge jolted through my body.

With that big flower petal across my mouth, I couldn't even scream. The petals heated up around my head. It felt like little needles were jabbing into my brain.

Every one of the tentacles that held me tight heated up, too. Energy pulsed and thrummed from them, spreading all through me.

I jerked around, tried to turn my head or free my arms and legs, but the chair held me too tight. No matter how much I struggled, I couldn't escape.

CHAPTER 16

"Okay! That's enough for today," Brad said cheerfully from behind me.

The chair stopped thrumming and cooled off. Then the tentacles and the flower let go of me.

I sat there. No way could I move. I felt like I'd been run over by a steamroller.

"Hey, come take a look," Brad said. He leaned over the grow tank.

My body couldn't resist Brad's order. I got to my feet and stumbled over to where Brad stood. I kind of fell against the tank.

It was full of murky brown liquid and dim light. I could just make out, floating in the center, a vaguely human shape.

Brad patted my head. "Good job. Let's go home!"

Easy for him to say.

I did my best to follow him, but I fell twice just trying to get up the basement stairs.

He came back and helped me up. He put his arm around my shoulders and helped me walk all the way to the other house. "I must have left you in the chair a little too long," he muttered. "Gotta watch that tomorrow."

Tomorrow?

What did he mean, *tomorrow*? I couldn't do that again! I wouldn't. I had to find a way out of this!

"In the meantime you've got to get your strength up!" Brad told me. "I bet you're hungry!" He helped me to a kitchen chair, then ran upstairs.

I heard him talking to the rest of my family, and pretty soon they all came downstairs, blinking but looking happy and well rested. Mom started making a big dinner. Brad, Tyler, and Alex watched TV, and Dad went out to get the paper.

Mom made lots of all my favorite foods. I thought I was too tired to eat, until Brad said, "Go on, Randi. Eat up!"

I moved my fork from my plate to my mouth. I could barely taste the food, I was eating so fast.

"Had enough?" he asked.

My stomach *hurt* it was so full of food. "Uh-huh," I said, my mouth stuffed with lasagna.

"You can stop now."

For a minute I felt grateful to him.

Tyler stared from me to Brad and back. "Brad, you're being so weird. Why do you care how much Randi eats?"

"I don't want her to get sick," Brad told my twin. "I care about her."

"Awww." A goofy look crossed Tyler's face.

I so wanted to tell him the truth—tell him Brad only cared about having me as a human blueprint! But I also didn't want to fall on the floor in one of those painful coughing fits! I decided to keep my mouth shut—for now.

After dinner Brad wished me a very special good night. "Sleep well," he whispered from the doorway after I'd brushed my teeth and crawled into bed. "Rest up. Get strong! Sweet dreams."

The next day I wondered if it hadn't all been a dream. I got up and felt a hundred percent better than I had when I went to bed. Everybody was cheerful. Brad acted friendly.

He still wore Tyler's baseball cap, and he had on a long-sleeved shirt instead of his rugby shirt, something stretchy of Tyler's, and shorts. He also still wore that pendant.

Not a dream, I realized. Definitely not a dream. After breakfast Brad commanded me and Tyler to race around chasing a ball with him.

"I got it! I got it!" Brad yelled to us. He tripped on a rock and fell.

When he stood up, he left some of his leg behind.

I gasped and pointed to the long red-brown strip of skin dangling from his leg.

Brad glanced around. Tyler had his back to us, and Alex was looking the other way, too.

Brad ran inside. He came back a little later wearing jeans and gloves.

After lunch he made my family take another nap. And Brad and I went back to the basement in the vacant house.

I ran over to the tank when we got there.

The water still looked a little murky, but the form in it seemed more solid. Definitely human-shaped. No more ground round or T-bone steaks or raw eggs or fertilizer floating around in the soup.

The murk cleared a bit, and I made out a skin-less face. Eyeballs stared up from nests of raw red muscles with nerves and veins snaking over them.

Then, while I watched, the eyeballs rolled sideways. They stared right into my eyes!

My heart pounded in my chest.

The creature looked at me.

It was *alive*!

CHAPTER 17

"Cool, huh?" Brad said. "It's coming together nicely!"

"I—I—" I stuttered. Even with all the amazing instruments Brad had, I never thought his scheme would work. But it *was working!* There really was a human body forming, in that tank!

"Have a seat," Brad said. He jerked his thumb toward the big pink chair.

Noooo, I moaned in my head. I never wanted to sit in that chair again!

Brad's powers forced me to climb up into it anyway. My eyes remained glued to the strange body forming in the tank. I sat still while the chair grabbed me with tentacles and the blue flower.

When Brad flipped the switch, I didn't try to struggle. It would all be over soon, I told myself.

When he switched off the machine this time, I felt totally drained of *all* energy.

He leaned on the grow tank. "Good body," he whispered to the thing inside. "Good body!"

This time Brad practically had to lift me out of the chair and carry me back to our house.

I noticed the skin on his cheek was beginning to peel off, too. Brad's condition was getting worse, I realized. Soon he'd switch into his new body and get rid of me!

But I wouldn't let that happen. An idea was forming in my head. One that might actually get rid of Brad—for good.

He came to dinner with an Ace bandage wrapped around part of his face—and nobody said anything! He used the pendant to make my family see what he wanted them to see.

I ate another big dinner, which made Brad happy.

Good, I thought. *Smile away, Brad. Because I have a plan. One you're not going to like.*

I only hope that it works.

Instead of lying down in bed, I stuffed pillows under my sheet. Then I hid in the closet. When Brad peeked into my room, I shut my eyes and stopped my ears with my fingers. Brad muttered something, but I didn't hear it this time.

Yes! Brad thought he had given me a sleep order, but I hadn't heard it. Hadn't seen the light of the glistening pendant. I was free. At least until morning.

One more session in that pink chair, and I was going to die. I just knew it.

If I was going to save my life, I had to do it now. Before it was too late!

CHAPTER 18

I thought over the commands Brad had given me. Was there any way around them?

Okay. I had to obey Brad. I couldn't tell anybody he was an alien, or anything about his plans. I couldn't shrink him.

What *could* I do?

Well, Brad didn't say I couldn't run away, I realized. I could go someplace far away—someplace where he couldn't find me.

But how would I live? Eat? Sleep?

And what if Brad put Tyler in the pink chair instead of me? He had my whole family hypnotized with that pendant. He could suck the life out of Tyler just as easily as he did it to me.

No. I couldn't run. I had to stop Brad!

I snuck down the stairs and out the back door as quietly as I could. No sign of Brad.

I found a rock and broke the window of the vacant house's kitchen door, then reached inside and unlocked it.

After carefully investigating, I realized that Brad was nowhere to be found. I tiptoed down into the basement.

I tapped Brad's light globe, and it spread its eerie green light over everything. The pink chair's tentacles lay quiet. The power pack hummed in the silence.

The grow tank, I thought. I ran to it to check out Brad's new body.

The water wasn't murky anymore—I could see the body inside clearly. It had skin and hair in all the right places. It appeared alive, just sleeping.

In this body Brad would no longer resemble a blond California surfer boy. The new body looked more like me and Tyler.

It had curly brown hair. And its face had the same nose and mouth as Tyler's, the same eyebrows as my face.

It could be our triplet.

Or maybe just Tyler's new twin, once I was out of the way.

That was Brad's plan all along. Randi out, Brad in. No way! I thought. He can't have my family! I am not going to leave them.

I jerked loose the cords that connected the tank to the power pack and the pink chair. I found a bank of colored squares at one end of the tank. I punched the squares furiously—maybe I could wreck the machine. If I did, Brad would have no body to switch into…and no time to make a new one!

Colored light flashed through the liquid in the tank. I saw sparks shooting off the tank's other end. A burning smell invaded my nose.

Good! I was wrecking something!

My plan was working!

I punched more of the colored squares. Fizzing and hissing noises sounded; the wires embedded in the tank's side flashed.

A small round window opened in the end of the tank near me, and clear thick liquid poured out onto the basement floor.

I held my nose. Ugh! Sewage, fertilizer, mildew! A combination of the worst smells imaginable. I danced around to keep the goo from soaking my feet.

Then the tank lid popped open.

The body inside lay limp on the bottom of the tank.

Okay! Now I was getting somewhere! I stepped back and turned away. I didn't want to watch that body shrivel and die.

A horrible sloshing noise sounded in my ears.

What was happening?

I had to look.

I turned—and screamed!

The body stood up in the tank, its eyes wide and solid white. Its mouth hung open. Clear jellylike goo dripped down its face, chest, and arms. It turned this way and that—sniffing—like a dog trying to find a scent.

"Uh…uh…" it grunted.

It took some deep sniffing breaths, then leaned forward. It fell out of the tank with a horrible *splosh* on the hard cement floor.

Then it staggered to its feet.

And came shambling toward me, its arms outstretched!

Oh, no! That horrible thing was coming for me! It was going to kill me!

I headed for the basement stairs, but I was still so weak! I didn't have any speed!

The monster's sticky footsteps sounded right behind me.

I lunged for the stairs—too late! The monster's cold, wet hands wrapped around my throat!

CHAPTER 19

I tugged at the monster's warm, gooey hands. No use! It was too strong! I struggled for breath, but the monster held tight—tighter.

Black spots swam before my eyes. No! I thought. This is it. I'm a goner!

The body released its grip.

I sucked in a breath. Air! Oh, air! I thought.

The thing grabbed my shoulders. "Uh! Uh, uh, uh!" it said, shaking me. Then it patted my hair, touched my back.

I turned to look at it.

In its weird white eyes, pale gray irises formed. Black pupil dots floated in their centers.

"Uh?" it asked. It patted my cheek with one of its sticky, sour-smelling hands, then touched my mouth. "Uh?"

Maybe it didn't want to kill me.

Maybe it just didn't know what I was!

"It's okay," I muttered in a hoarse voice. My throat still hurt. "It's okay, it's okay."

It blinked and calmed down. "Uh…uh…"

I patted its head.

Its drooping mouth closed and curved up into a sloppy smile. One that looked a lot like Tyler's.

It put its arms around me and hugged.

Kind of hard, but not painfully.

Whoa. Strange.

Chills pimpled my arms. Hair prickled on the back of my neck. This was almost too weird to think about.

The thing touched my cheek, and I touched his. He made a crooning, gurgling sound, and he looked happy.

I patted him on the head some more. "Good boy! Good monster."

"Uh," he mumbled, smiling again.

Then I realized. He didn't know *anything*. In the tank he looked like a sleeping person, but now I realized he was a giant baby. He didn't know what I was saying, and he couldn't talk.

Brad could *try* to use that pendant on him and order him around, but how could you give orders to something that didn't understand you?

"Goo monser," he said.

"Good monster," I repeated. Then I thought, no! I shouldn't teach him any words! Then Brad will be able to control him.

Hey! Maybe I could teach *him* to grab Brad's pendant! I couldn't grab it because Brad was able to control me. But if Brad couldn't control this body...

I ran to the shelf where Brad left the rest of the alien stuff he took out of the off-limits closet. I searched through all the boxes.

So many tiny machines. I tapped the black patch on some of them, growing them one stage. I had no idea what they did, and now every single one of them was kind of frightening.

I came across a diamond-shaped pink thing that looked a little like Brad's hypnopendant, attached to a thin black cord. I knotted the cord and slipped the pendant around my neck.

The monster followed me to the shelves. He pawed through the boxes, too. "Uh, uh." He frowned. He tried to eat a green disk. I grabbed it out of his mouth before he swallowed it.

Who knew what this stuff would do in someone's stomach?

I led the monster over to the stairs.

I decided I would teach him one word: "Take."

I patted his shoulder, then grabbed his hand and dragged him down to sit next to me on the bottom stair.

He nudged me with his shoulder and grinned with his mouth half open.

Like a big *puppy*!

I took one of the monster's hands and closed it around my pink pendant. "Take," I said. I wrapped my hands around his and lifted the pendant up and off me. Then I let go of his hand.

The monster opened his hand and stared at the pink thing.

Then he tried to lick it.

"No," I said, pulling his hand away from his mouth. I took the pendant back from him and put it around my neck again. "Take," I said.

I closed his hand over it and lifted it so he took the pendant off my neck without strangling me. I released his hand.

He stared at me for a long moment, then opened his hand to look at the pendant. He didn't try to lick it this time.

I took it back from him and started all over.

It didn't take him long to figure it out.

I patted his shoulder, and he gave me a big goofy grin.

We rehearsed some more until I was sure he knew what I meant.

I was so tired by the time we finished that just sitting up exhausted me.

The monster looked really tired, too.

But at least I had a plan, and a helper.

I led the monster around the other side of the furnace and settled him on the floor. He'd be safe there for the time being, I figured. I patted his head, and soon he fell asleep. I settled a tarp from the basement floor over him like a blanket.

I thought about Brad's plans to take over the monster with his consciousness.

I didn't know the monster very well, but I liked him lots more than I liked Brad.

If the monster would only do what we practiced, we would be saving *both* our lives.

I closed the tank and hooked it back up to the power pack and the pink chair, so it would look undisturbed. There wasn't much I could do about the sour smell in the air or the big wet spot on the floor, though.

I made my way back to the house.

The trap was set. Now all I had to do was get to my room before Brad realized I had been gone all night.

I reached the stairs and glanced up. I sucked in a breath.

Brad!

He was sitting on the stairs waiting for me.

And he was *not* happy.

CHAPTER 20

"Where have you been?" he cried.

I blinked at him.

His body was totally covered up: socks, long pants; long-sleeved shirt, gloves; a bandanna on top of his head under Tyler's baseball cap; and another bandanna covering the bottom of his face. All I could see of him were his eyes.

"Where *were* you? Tell me right now!" he yelled. He fumbled with the pendant around his neck.

Sparks of colored light darted around the room.

I couldn't let him focus that thing on me!

What if he made me tell him all about the monster, and the training, and…

I turned and staggered out of the house.

Brad came after me.

I heard him stumbling a few paces behind me. I glanced over my shoulder.

He wasn't in much better shape than I was. He dragged one foot behind him.

For a minute I thought about running out into the street and trying to flag someone down.

But there weren't any cars. It was too early in the morning.

I took a deep breath and ran to the vacant house.

Brad was right behind me as I lurched down the stairs to the basement. He grabbed my shoulder when we reached the floor and spun me around.

"Hey!" he yelled. "Where do you think you're going?"

I shoved him. My hand sank into his chest as though it were cookie dough. Ugh! He was turning to mush! My stomach heaved.

"*Oof!*" Brad coughed from the blow. He tried to grab me again. I headed toward the furnace.

Brad grabbed my wrist and spun me around. The pink pendant shone in his other hand. He aimed its lights toward my eyes.

Brad scowled at me. He held the pink pendant up from its place around his neck. He shone it in my eyes. "Since you're here and I'm here, we might as well complete this operation. I can't wait much longer anyway. It will kill you, but no matter. I need that body!"

He shoved me toward the pink chair. "Say goodbye to your world, Randi. You're about to leave it—forever!"

CHAPTER 21

I glanced over Brad's shoulder. I had only one hope—the monster. Was he awake?

Yes! He was! Over Brad's shoulder, I could see him shambling toward us.

Would he remember our plan?

I smiled at him.

Brad noticed my expression. He whirled and saw the monster. "No!" he screamed. "Nooo!"

I struggled to pull free from Brad's grip. "Monster!" I yelled. "Take!"

The monster stretched his goofy mouth into a smile and came closer. He looked at my chest.

No! Not there! I thought. Please, this has to work!

"Monster! Take!" I yelled over Brad's screams. I pointed to Brad. "Take! Take!"

The monster reached out and ripped the pendant out of Brad's hand.

"Good monster!" I yelled.

Brad let go of my arm. He grabbed the monster's hand, trying to free the pendant from his grip.

The monster lifted the pendant high, trying to lift it over Brad's head the way I had taught him. But the string it was on was really strong. It hooked under Brad's chin.

The monster couldn't figure out why the pendant didn't slip off of Brad. He dragged it this way and that, pulling Brad's body, flopping him right and left as if he were a rag doll.

Brad fell to the floor. His scarves and hat fell off in the struggle.

Ugh. Most of Brad's skin was peeling off his bones. I gagged. He looked like a zombie—a rotting corpse from a horror movie now.

The monster put a foot on Brad's head to hold him still, then he jerked the pendant off him.

Yes! I knew he was smart!

He brought the pendant straight to me.

"Good boy!" I grabbed the pendant, then gave the monster a hug.

"Uh, uh," he said, and hugged me back, a little too hard.

I held up the pendant. Held it up and shone its light in Brad's eyes. "You have no power over me anymore!" I said. "Now I control you! You can't get up from the floor—ever! You can't get up from the floor!" I repeated.

"Raaaaandi." Brad's disintegrating mouth moaned the word.

He lay on the floor, twitching. A shudder passed over him. His features blurred. His body was totally breaking down.

"I liked this planet," he whispered. His human face began to melt away, revealing his hideous lizard head.

"All I ever wanted was to stay here," he said.

He twitched again violently. Then his body disintegrated, melting into a pile of ashes.

CHAPTER 22

Brad was gone. But he had built the monster's body to last.

I glanced at the monster. He smiled at me. I couldn't help smiling back. He liked me! He really liked me.

I shook out Brad's clothes and taught the monster how to put them on.

He learned fast.

I found the black touch pads on the grow tank, the power pack, and the pink chair. I unplugged everything from everything else, and shrank the alien machines until they fit neatly into the cardboard boxes.

The monster helped me carry the boxes back to our house. We put them into the upstairs closet.

The monster needed a shower, for sure, and something to eat. I could use something myself.

I taught the monster how to eat cereal and milk. He really liked Frosted O's, and I only had to show him how to use a spoon one time.

Soon he'd be a full-fledged human, I thought. He smiled at me through a mouth full of Frosted O's.

Hmm. How could I get Mom and Dad to adopt him? I wondered. I clutched Brad's pink pendant in my hand. I'd watched Brad operate it often enough…

A smile spread across my face. I slung my arm around the monster's shoulders.

Yup. No doubt about it. Tyler and I were going to love having a triplet.

ABOUT THE AUTHOR

Photograph © Dan Nelken

R.L. (Robert Lawrence) Stine is one of the best-selling children's authors in history. His Goosebumps series, along with such series as Fear Street, The Nightmare Room, Rotten School, and Mostly Ghostly have sold nearly 400 million books in this country alone. And they are translated into 32 languages.

The *Goosebumps* TV series was the top-rated kids' series for three years in a row. R.L.'s TV movies, including *The Haunting Hour: Don't Think About It* and *Mostly Ghostly*, are perennial Halloween favorites. And his scary TV series, *R.L. Stine's The Haunting Hour*, is in its second season on The Hub network.

R.L. continues to turn out Goosebumps books, published by Scholastic. In addition, his first horror novel for adults in many years, titled *Red Rain*, will be published by Touchstone books in October 2012.

R.L. says that he enjoys his job of "scaring kids." But the biggest thrill for him is turning kids on to reading.

R.L. lives in New York City with his wife, Jane, an editor and publisher, and King Charles Spaniel, Minnie. His son, Matthew, is a sound designer and music producer.